MW01602624

Christian Wingrove-Rogers – **Clay Tree Bird**

Christian Wingrove–Rogers

CLAY TREE BIRD

Flash Fiction, Poetry and Photography

PalmArtPress
Berlin

For Kerstin…

… who is often wonderful.

Thank you for twenty years of sharing words.

Before Words

This is a collection of seven stories and seven frag-mented poems. They were all written during spring, summer and autumn of twenty-twenty, a period of time in which, when the future looks back, will be referred to by a name that has yet to be decided. The words in this collection were not written as a result of this period, but they were undoubtedly affected by it. Apart from two of the stories, *The Pact* and *The Well*, everything in this book was written or photographed within walking distance of the wooden wagon in a field in Brandenburg where I live. All of the words were written under the influence of freshly foraged wild herbs, hot water and honey.

The title *Clay Tree Bird* has no deeper meaning other than that it presented itself while I was looking out my window one morning and saw a bird perched on the edge of a terracotta flower pot. The bird then flew up to look for bugs on the branches of the walnut tree. Out of this moment one of the stories was conceived—whilst reading you will discover which one.

I hope these words and images give as much pleasure as they gave me in finding and writing them.

Christian Wingrove-Rogers
Schönfelde October 24, 2020

In the silence I hear
In the darkness I see

But I will never
get my mind around

The immensity of a tree

Preface

The rising sun shines over an enchanted land.

The trees shudder, as if over them passes the soul of the earth, ascending through the gate of the sun's knowledge. The grass and the flowers nestled within it, the bush and the hedge are all regaled with their true colour. The birds sing at the sun's arrival.

Nature speaks her message. She does not whisper. Her voice is not constrained by intonation, jargon or attitude; unlike religion, it is clear and free. The message she bears is not unfathomable, riddled with mystery, nor spoken in tongues. It is not gleaned from a hidden knowledge obscured by the depths of time whose intention was, and still is, to fill the listener with a wistful yearning for the past. Nor does it play on the fear of one's inadequacy.

Nature does not bear a message through suffering, and neither does she frame it within a gilded vision.

For that is not the language nature speaks. Hers is not a language whose intention is to keep us removed from truth but, by speaking directly to the self, for us to become truth.

'Beauty is truth, truth beauty,' – *that is all ye know on earth, and all ye need to know.* Keats wrote this for us—so we have been told—and there is no excuse for not knowing. This is the message then of nature—speaking a language we can all understand—and it is simple: truth, like beauty, is eternal; for those who learn to live with it, peace, likewise eternal, will endure.

We cannot be further from truth but, each new day, we can be closer to it.

THE CLAY

One warm, late-summer afternoon, sitting beneath a tree in a garden, a potter was preparing to throw a lump of clay onto the wheel in front him. His bare right foot, swaying gently back and forth, measured the resistance of a larger wheel at the base of a vertical axle that turned another higher, smaller wheel before him. On the bench beside him lay a damp cloth. The only tools he had, or needed, were his hands.

The tree was wide and sprawling. The potter liked to work there, as he had plenty of room to move around, and the shade protected him from the sun. Sitting there brought back memories of being in the village church as a child; instead of being enclosed by symbols of death and images suffering, there under the tree, the potter was surrounded with life. The tree was old, and one or two of the lower branches were no longer alive. The potter would never cut them out, because he did not want to disturb anything. Thus, beneath the loosened bark of one of those branches, a host of insects had made their home. As he contemplated the clay, a fragment of the bark fell onto the wheel. He looked up and saw the bare section of the branch and the insects scrambling about looking for a place to hide. He smiled and turned back to his wheel. He did not think to move, because he knew that by sitting there he would not be bothered by falling bark again. There was none left to fall.

His focus returned to the turning wheel. Then, onto it, he threw the lump of clay.

From another limb of the same tree, a young bird was eyeing the feast, scuttling around the branch above the potter's head. The bird was eager to feed but was also wary of the human presence and the danger that might mean. His tail quivered as he bobbed up and down 'tut-tutting' in agitation. He seemed to be measuring the distance to and back from his meal. Alternately, the bird observed the man and then the insects. He was caught in a quandary. And he was hungry.

The potter, whilst being aware of the bird with its impatient, juvenile twittering, concentrated on turning the wheel, the rhythm of which seemed to calm the bird a little. The mass of clay found its form. The potter paid no heed to anything but his commitment; the bond between the earth and his hands which moved, seeking not to simply impose his will and form the clay, but rather to seek its form. He sought the points that required a gentler touch and those where they should be firm. The clay, working through the unhurrying hands of the potter, began to take the shape of a low, almost perfectly round bowl.

The bird, realising that the man was fully absorbed in his task and consequently harmless, suddenly spread his wings. A short flight, dipping almost to the man's shoulder, took him across to the dead branch. The feast was his.

Directly below, mindful of the bird's presence and closeness, the potter did not react in any way. He quietly held the rhythm of the turning wheel, to which the tap-tap-tapping of the bird taking the insects seemed to resonate. The potter's slippery, wet hands on the side of the bowl rose up as if they were proffering a gift up to the far-sky above and beyond the tree.

And for a while the bird and the potter remained, separated by their own intentions, held in the same dimension, woven in a shared existence.

An insect fell onto the lip of the bowl. The potter carefully, with the nail of his little finger, removed and set it on the ground beside him. The bird, disturbed by the movement, the change in circumstance, flew out of the tree and was gone. The potter heard its wings hitting the air, sounding like that of someone in the distance shaking out a cloth.

When he saw that the bowl could not be improved upon, the potter stared at it for a while. More than satisfied; he was happy. He placed it in the sun to dry.

THE TREE

When a young gardener had finished the work of planting some saplings, he found that there was one for which he found no place. It was weak looking and its branches thin. One had snapped off, leaving a rough-edged stump. The gardener had casually set the sturdier trees first, leaving the smaller ones until last, so to plant them where they were less likely to be seen. Not caring much to find a place for the broken, leftover sapling; he had left it lying on the edge of the river bank where he had been taking a rest from his back-aching work. When he got up to go, he had forgotten about it.

The river flowed quietly along.

At the top of the slope, where on hot days children ran down to reach the river, was an old Oak. It had been standing there for longer than anyone could remember.

When the wind came, it caused the uppermost branches of the tree to sway and its leaves to dance. The tree was proud to be standing there at the top of the slope, and through the wind, which carried its thoughts, it said so.

The roots of the forgotten sapling had done their work. They had settled into the moist, welcoming soil and had taken hold of the ground upon which the young tree lay. Time, with the help of the sun and the same wind that caressed the Oak, had hauled the sapling upright. Now it stood proudly, watching the water flow past its feet. The water, like the wind, whispered comforting thoughts to the growing tree.

On pleasant days, when grey-haired men wearing caps came with their easels and canvases to gaze at and sketch it, the Oak was especially proud.

"How magnificent I am. The eyes of so many turn to me and find joy in my presence. See how they study me, replicating my majesty, the memory of which they take away to keep. Only I am treated this way. I must be the most marvellous and worthy of all trees."

The other trees heard these thoughts in the wind, which carried them far and wide.

Now quite grown up, the tree on the riverbank listened with interest. The Oak began to make parallels between them. It considered the river, made unruly by reeds and weeds, more impoverished compared to its own smooth grassy slope. It mocked the crabby little fruit that grew on the branches of the tree. Fruit that nobody would eat because they were sour. As far as the Oak was concerned that common little tree that clung to the riverbank was insignificant and worthless. It, the Oak, was majestic and of far greater value. Believing that it was as much a part of the sky as the sun and the moon, it feared nothing.

One day a tempestuous storm came. The rain lashed down from clouds as dark as night. A wind unknown to that land tore through the landscape, and the mighty Oak, standing steadfast and firm was damaged. Its rigid branches snapped and fell, shifting its weight, which cracked and split its mighty trunk.

Before the eye of the storm, the tree on the river bank had felt its strength, but instead of straining against a power over which it had no influence, it had allowed itself to bend in the wind. Thus, when the storm passed, the tree stood upright once more. It did not break.

The next day the river flowed serenely again, caressing the feet of the tree on the riverbank.

The Bird

The stillness of the night that had seemed endless was about to break with the calls of a thousand chattering birds.

The sky was brightening, changing colour from indigo to a lush cerulean blue, streaked with strains of honey, which always accompanied the arrival of the sun.

One of those birds, alone on a rooftop, was waiting— not for the sun but the wind.

Having left the cold summits of the mountains, and having passed over the tree-tops of the forests, the wind had grown weary. Coming to the city, its strength much faded, the wind rippled the surface of the qanat. There women were already collecting the daily water before passing through the gateway and down the narrow alleyways, bringing a freshness to the houses and the small shops. It shook the dust from the wares hanging in the souk and made the embroidered silken flowers on the curtains of the Sultan's palace dance. The wind did not discriminate.

In its beak, the bird held a seed.

As the wind saw the bird perched atop the roof of the house, where the poet, a seller of words lived, it paused. At that moment it forgot that its destination—not its final destination, for that it did not know—was beyond the city walls.

The bird turned its face to the oncoming wind, transferred the seed to one of its claws, and took to the air.

"Take me with you."
"Do you know where I am going?"
"I do not."
"Then why do you ask to go with me."
"I have a responsibility. I have a seed that I must sow, and this is not the place."
"How do you know that I will take you to the right place."
"I trust you."

The wind turned toward the city wall and passed over it with the bird on its shoulder. Together they passed over the oasis at the edge of the city and beyond—into the desert. The wind shook off its mantle of mountain cold and grew warm. The bird, with its eyes half-closed, found a thermal within the wind and settled upon it. Below them, sand skipped and swirled into the air as they passed.

"What is the seed?"
"I do not know."

"Where does it come from?"
"I do not know that either."
"But who gave it to you?"
"Nor do I know that."

The wind, the bird and the seed came to a dry unforgiving place where nothing moved.

"Here."
The bird softly landed on the dusty ground and with care put the seed into it. The wind, unwilling and unable to remain, continued its journey with a sigh that only the bird recognised.
The bird lay down and slept.
But wind does not forget. It often passed over the bird and the seed bringing with it rain.

One day when it returned, the tender leaves of a small tree shook at its arrival but not the feathers of the bird. It was as if life had passed from one to the other.
Like time, the wind, cannot stand still. Blowing through and over the branches of the beautiful tree, the wind saw perched among them a small brown bird. It held, in its beak, a seed.

The Pact

It always happens like this on a threshold: an edge where one place ends and another begins.

Stand at a border and you may decide where you wish to go or to belong ... which side you will take.

Even if for some reason you think that you cannot, you will still take a decision.

It is like being at a fork in a road.

Look in one direction and you will know that there is another.

The sun, in the chalk-blue sky, was not yet at its strongest, having only just risen above the hills beyond the city.

A girl came to a shallow but wide watering hole, a well that was nestled in the trees of a small wood. She had with her a clay jar, which she set down at her feet, then untying her headscarf she shook her hair free of confinement. She stood quite still for a moment to breath in the cool air that rose from the water. Then she turned her attention to her task. The well. She laughed, seeing the wet colours dancing there. She began to sing;

the words to her song were her thoughts. The sun's lamp lit upon the clear water, and on its surface she saw her likeness as one does in a dream—and as in a dream, she was pleased. Seeing the image of her face, she saw that her skin was dark, perhaps a shade too dark from working so long in her fathers field. Her eyes were very round and strong, which showed her confidence, even as they betrayed her innocence. Her mother called them her questioning eyes. They were eyes that beguiled.

She could see her smile.

Her image found favour. She saw her self.

Not wishing for the enchantment to fall away, she did not move.

Truth held.

But truth, as a mirror, we have an uneasy pact with. A deal that can be broken.

There is always an image we may or may not care to see. A vision that is open to influence.

She thrust her jar in, shattering the surface of the illusion. The image of her self disappeared.

The shocked water simmered and foamed, and in each foaming bit a new body took shape. One face became a hundred. Each bearing a barely perceptible image of her. She could not concentrate on, or bring into focus one, without her attention being snared by another. It was like a game, trying to catch sight of an image of her self before its bubble burst. Again she laughed.

From across the water, the muffled sound of rippling waves echoed back to her. From the trees of the wood came her laughter.

As she pulled up the jar, leaning over to find out how much water it bore, she saw her smile coming up to meet her.

She tucked her hair in and under her scarf, wrapped it back on, picked up the jar now full, and turned to leave. But she could not.

She stared into the distance; she waited for the water to settle.

Before she left, giving thanks to the well, she looked down at its surface again and saw her reflection.
Now she could leave. She could only bear one truth.

Just one.

The Well

He was walking. It was early, and the day was fine. Dew still clung to the thorn bushes and lay over the few thin patches of grass that the mountain goats had missed. The town was not so far behind him, and he could still hear its sounds. He even imagined that he could smell its smells. A cowering dog with matted fur and strangely long legs had followed him, even though he had given it no encouragement. The poet had no food to give and no desire to disappoint the poor creature. But still it had accompanied him, as if they were both bound together on the same journey. The path was empty and, unlike in the bustling alleys of the city, he could set his own pace. A pace which encouraged thought.

He had walked long enough to lose the stiffness in his back that the night spent on a strange mattress had given him, and now he hoped for a place to sit and be calm. He came to a small coppice of trees, in the middle of which was a watering place. The surface of the water was just below ground level, and being dark he judged it to be deep. At one end there was a low wall, into which two wooden benches had been built on, and where the water gatherers could put their containers.

He sat down on one of them, closed his eyes and listened. He heard only the wind that brought word from the mountain, and he felt only the bench beneath him. The measure of his breathing joined that of the wind. His thoughts followed one another into a poem which would never be spoken.

When he opened his eyes he found that he was not alone.

How long she had been there he could not tell.

At the far end of the well, a woman was gazing into the water, laughing and singing. Lit by the lamp of the sun, whose beams danced through the branches and across the clear surface of the water, he could see what she could see. Her likeness, as if in a dream, appeared to float upon it. She seemed pleased, finding pleasure in her image. His eyes moved from the reflection and up to her. Believing herself to be alone, she wore no scarf. She had short hair that shined like an obsidian mirror. Her skin, glorious in the sunlight, was of a tone that seemed to imitate, but not equal, the radiance of a band of gold on her wrist. Her eyes, round and sweet, expressed the purity of her thoughts. Her expression made him feel faint. She waved her hand above her own reflection, moving with the grace of a pearl of water running down the surface of a slender leaf. She was as unaware of his presence as he had been of her arrival. He dared not disturb this charming moment and remained stock still. Mesmerised by the speckled reflections the water cast on her face, all thoughts left him. Only the unspoken poem remained.

But such fleeting moments, like truth, do not last.

She plunged her jar into the water, breaking both the reflection and the enchantment. She held it under the surface, watching as it filled, and then, as she pulled it back up, he saw her smile again. She laughed and threw her head back and up to the sky; her black hair shimmered like the coat of one of the half wild horses the people of the mountains kept. She rested the jar on the ground beside her and, putting her scarf over her head, she waited for the water to settle. When it did, she turned to thank it. At that moment she could have seen either him, or his reflection, but if she had she did not react.

The poet did not move.

Then she was gone.

He could hardly believe that she had existed in the first place, and he was less inclined to do so now.

He went down to the waters edge to where the splashed water had soaked into the earth. He saw her footprints; she had been barefoot and, looking into the water, he saw what she had seen. The bronze-green surface of the well showed him, plainly and without deceit, a reflection of the self.

The Lake

It was evening. They sat by the lake at one of the short wooden jetties used by the village fishermen, of which there were now only a few; this meant that the landing places were no longer maintained. The planks were dodgy, and the undergrowth along the bank, from which the rickety structures reached out into the water, was overgrown. They were a perfect place to swim from and to ignore, and be ignored by, humans. Theirs was number seven, but the number had fallen off.

Diving in, she led the way, and together they swam out to where the sun could see them. They splashed around for a while, like children; then floating on their backs within a hands reach of one another, each sought their own thoughts. They admired the season-changed aspects of the trees and the shifting formations of clouds above them. Summer's fullness was fading. Then this time, with him leading the way, they returned to the little jetty. Naked under a shared woollen blanket, and with silent words they sat watching the ducks pass, while they drank tea from a thermos. The air was not cold but cool. The sunlight still found ways through the branches and leaves of the enormous oak tree under which they sat. As always, they were thankful for nature and felt privileged to be able to be with it and each other. She would always say this, and he would always smile.

The surface of the water, aside the trails left by the ducks, was like a sheet of polished steel into which a few curled leaves and acorn cups, like jewels in a crown, had been set. Its colour, further out in the pale sunshine, was a dark silvery green, whilst below the trees it was a shade of slate grey. The peace and the stillness took their breath.

So they didn't lob acorns into the water and, trying to imitate it, laugh at the plopping sound that they made—as they usually would. But they did gently drop the cupules in, which looked like a line of little coracles whilst floating away.

Then they saw the weather change, and with it the season.

They knew it would come, the change, they had felt it. That was why they had gone there. One last time until the next year. That is what had made it all the more important. It was a day not to hold on to or to take for granted like other sunny days; there had been many that summer. It was a moment in time like no other, a moment to witness and to embrace.

The gust of wind had been unexpected but not sudden. They had heard it coming. The trees at the far end of the lake had called out its presence, and the reeds had rustled around them in warning. Though light and without drama, the wind, with so many trees around, was, as well as audible, very visible. Everything, it seemed, was holding its breath as the wind approached.

Then they could see it. It came down the lake in a sweeping chevron of ripples that disturbed the mirror before them. The ducks lowered their necks and faced into it. They imagined that the fish were descending to the bed of the lake away from its now turbulent surface.

A chill cut through the damp cloth of the blanket, and they drew closer together.

Bearing the breath of autumn, the restless wind sweeping down the valley of trees and water changed everything it touched. It whipped the reeds into a chaotic frenzy out of which flew small brown birds. Perhaps fearing danger a swarm of Hornets left their nest high up in a hollow in the oak tree, coming out to stand guard at its entrance. The trees shivered, as did the pair under their blanket. A shower of acorns, a barrage of seed bombs, fell down through the branches around them onto the wooden jetty and into the water. They pulled the blanket up over their heads. One landed in the porcelain cup in her hand, making a sound so out of place that it made them laugh.

Then it was gone.

The wind, now no more than an echo, a rumour from further down its path, continued its journey.

They took one last swim in the water, each urging the other out toward the sight of the setting sun, to the West and the wind travelling through the trees to the East. Then they sat in the now cooler air until their bodies were dry. They dressed and went home.

Walking back through the forest, they didn't need words to show that they were grateful ... for everything.

Squirrel

My wooden wagon home on a border
    of a garden and a field
    that spreads to the horizon.
It is night
    the moon is full.
I try to sleep
    in my bed
    within a walnut tree
    which gives me the room to breath
The moon full
round and bright white
    lights the way to the bounty
    of nuts he seeks.
The squirrel throws them
    onto the roof above my head
    where they will roll down
    to the end of the bed
    and drop
    onto the glass morning table.
He is clever and wise
    practical
the harvest collects in one place.
I cannot sleep
with this going on
    so
    from my window
I watch
the hard rain that falls
    on this night of light.

Rain

The moss on the rock is wet
    pressing my finger into it I know
    how long it has rained

and it rains still.

Opening the door the warmth of my wagon embraces me
    the melancholy light makes the tea taste better.

I want to go out again
    to find someone to invite in

out of the rain.

Autumn I

An autumn wind will not whisper
    nor will it scream or lament
    but relentless
    it will crash against the trees
    snapping branches that cannot bear the winter
    for which it paves the way

In preparing the bare bones
    to stand still and naked in a field
    through months of cold
    and early darkness
    the wind's grip is not light
    each leaf it takes is hurled
    and twirled a thousand times

An autumn wind does nothing by half

It knows
    There is much to do
    in moving a season on
    for the start of a new year

Autumn II

The cranes
    all wings and legs
    struggle to land

When they do
    they are restless
    there is no peace
    when the wind is pulling
    at your feathers

They depart
    rising effortlessly
    into the sky
    they are grey
    against the grey of autumn

feeling the wind speed
    knowing
    by staying still
    too long
    they risk
    become other bare bones
    in a field

Bench I

For Rhiannon

A bench in the garden
 below the umbrella
 of a walnut tree

I promise, one day,
 I will take you there
 to sit, just to sit

beneath the umbrella
 of a tree tall
 enough to see the sea

BENCH II

The bench is old
    peeling paint flakes
    curling from the wood
    like petals in the rain

split staves warped
    through the slow summer
    are somehow still
    held fast

by gnarled bolts
    tempered by the turn of time

BENCH III

Nature's repossession
    is a gradual affair
    as reasonable as truth

or a promise

and like the bench
    below the walnut tree

where one day
    we will sit
    my promise
    will always stand

Bird

"Good morning." Said the bird

"Good morning." Said the sun

"I have been waiting for you." Said the bird

"Why?" Asked the sun

"To say good morning."

SUN

"Have you been waiting long."

"I have; I am always up before you."

"No." Said the sun.

"I get up earlier
  just somewhere else."

The Great Noise

Once, long ago, or perhaps not so long ago, in a deep green wood full of oak trees, there lived a scurry of squirrels. A scurry, I should tell you, is the collective name for a group of squirrels.

Now one day, while the others were enjoying the morning sunshine, which was pouring through the trees like honey from a spoon, one squirrel was gathering nuts until he heard a terrifying sound; this made him jump and scared him greatly. He dashed back to the other squirrels and caused them all to gather in a huddle.

"I have just heard a terrible sound! How frightening it was. We are in great danger, and we must run away."

The sound he had heard was, in fact, the crashing of an old tree that had fallen nearby. But he did not know this.

Such were the things that he said to the others as they stood gathered together, shaking in fear of what the noise might mean. They decided to run away.

As they ran, they passed a rabbit who asked them why they were running.

"We heard a terrible sound. We are terrified!" They said.

The rabbit reported this to the rest of his colony, which is what a group of rabbits is called.

They decided, as the squirrels were running from the terrible sound, that they too should do so. So they did.

As they ran after the squirrels, they passed a business of ferrets; a business is a collective name for ferrets, who called out to them.

"Where are you going in such a rush?"

"We heard a terrible noise. Terrifying!" The rabbits shouted as they ran.

The ferrets, who are easily scared, began to panic, and they too decided that the best thing to do would be to run.

As they ran, they passed a group of hedgehogs, which, as we all know, is known as an array of hedgehogs.

They too asked what the fuss was all about to which the ferrets replied.

"A terrible noise. A terrifying noise!"

The debate began within the array of hedgehogs, and it was deemed wise to follow the suit of the ferrets and run away.

They, in turn, passed a cete of badgers. I don't need to tell you that bunch of badgers is known as a cete, now do I?

"What's the panic for?" They asked.

"A noise! A terrifying noise! Run for your lives!"

The badgers did not need to be told twice. They ran.

They came to a skulk of foxes. Do I need to tell you? I am sure I do not. The foxes enquired as to the cause for alarm. The badgers told them.

"Noise! Terrible. Run!"

The foxes took flight immediately. They came to a group, a sounder of boar, who were happily snouting around in the ground.

"Hey ho foxes! What's the to do?"

"It's terrifying! Run."

Boar are generally slow on the uptake but not this time. They ran along in a cloud of dust which took them near to a parcel of deer. Yes, a parcel. Who asked the boar what was going on.

"Oh, it's terrifying. Run!"

Being cautious at the best of times the deer took to their heels.

They cantered along and out of the trees, where they saw all the other animals gathered together, looking quite anxiously back into the wood. At this point, a single solitary female wildcat, who was lying on a branch of a tree, called down to them.

"What on earth are you doing?" She enquired of the deer.

"It was so terrifying! We ran away."

"What was terrifying?"

"A noise."

"What noise?"

"The noise."

"Yes, but which noise?"

"The loud noise that was heard."

"Who heard?"

"We don't know, the boar told us about it."

"We will ask the boar then where this noise came from."

The wildcat turned to the sounder of boar, who were trembling in fear.

"Well, where did this sound come from, and what made it?"

"We don't know. The foxes told us about it."

The wildcat looked at the frightened skulk of foxes.

"Speak foxes. From where did this terrifying sound emanate?"

"We have no idea. The badgers told us to run. So we did. Ask them."

The wildcat did just that.

"You badgers there. Where did this sound happen?"

"How should we know? We heard about it from the hedgehogs."

The array of hedgehogs looked up at the wildcat.

"So? Where did this awful noise come from?"

"Ask the ferrets, they told us about it."

The wildcat turned to the business of fearful ferrets.

"What have you to say about this?"

"We know nothing. Nothing at all. The rabbits came pelting past us and told us that there had been a terrifying noise and that we should run. So we did. We ran, and here we are."

The rabbit colony had nothing to say on the matter other than to point at the scurry of squirrels.

"They told us to run. They told us that they had heard a really terrible noise."

"Is this true?" The wildcat asked of them.

"Sort of." They replied.

"So you know where this terrible sound came from."

"Actually, no. We didn't hear it ourselves. He did." They said, pointing to the one who had.

The wildcat sprang down from the branch in the tree and went up to one very small and abashed looking squirrel.

"So you know about this, do you? Where this sound, this terrible noise came from?"

"I do. I heard it while I was gathering nuts. Back in there." He pointed to the wood.

"Then," said the wildcat, "let us go and see what is so terrifying about it."

The animals all began to chatter at once.

"It will be dangerous."

"We might get eaten."

"It could be a big bad something or another."

"We don't want to die."

The wildcat looked at the assembly of creatures that had gathered around her.

"Between you all, you have claws and teeth, powerful muscles, strong bones and pointed antlers or tusks, yet you are scared of a noise! A noise that you know nothing about. Apart from one of you, of course, who has managed to get you all so frightened about something that you have not even heard, seen or smelt."

The animals were all beginning to look a little sheepish. The wildcat turned back to the squirrel.

"So now let us go and find out what it was that scared you. I am sure it cannot have been as bad as you have said."

The whole troupe of woodland animals marched along behind the wildcat and the squirrel.

The scurry, the colony, the business, the array, the cete, the skulk, the sounder and the parcel all stopped and stood in front of the place where the tree had fallen.

"Now, unless anyone is stupid enough to remain standing under a tree as it falls, how dangerous can a fallen tree be? It seems to me that your fear is more dangerous than that which caused it." Said the wildcat. She then turned to the squirrel. "As for you: you have taken fright at something, simply because you do not understand it. So now, all of you, just go away and carrying on with what you were doing."

The rabbits went back to being rabbits and the ferrets back to their business. There was an array of hedgehogs to be seen scuttling off into the leafy undergrowth, while the badgers set off to their cetes. The foxes were went skulking off to the edge of the wood and the sounder of boars, loudly, grunted away while rooting for roots. The deer went off in a parcel. The squirrels were all back up in the trees, and the one who had started the panic was scurrying off to his nuts.

The wildcat stretched herself out on a tree branch and tried to imagine a more stupid episode in the history of those woods. She couldn't.

The Last Star Of The Morning

When I saw it, I asked ...

What should I do today?

And it answered ...

Whatever you can

Bibliografische Information der Deutschen Nationalbibliothek
Die Deutsche Nationalbibliothek verzeichnet diese Publikation in der
Deutschen Nationalbibliografie; detaillierte bibliografische Daten sind
im Internet über www.dnb.de abrufbar.

ISBN: 978-3-96258-0

1. Auflage 2020, PalmArtPress, Berlin
Alle Rechte vorbehalten
© 2020 Christian Wingrove-Rogers

Palm**Art**Press
Verlegerin: Catharine J. Nicely
Pfalzburgerstr. 69, 10719 Berlin
www.palmartpress.com

Hergestellt in Deutschland